ADVENTURE TIME

GET ON THE MIC

PSS!
PRICE STERN SLOAN
An Imprint of Penguin Group (USA) Inc.

The publisher does not have any control over and does not assume any responsibility for author or third-party websites or their content.

ADVENTURE TIME, CARTOON NETWORK, the logos, and all related characters and elements are trademarks of and © Cartoon Network. (s13)

Published in 2013 by Price Stern Sloan, a division of Penguin Young Readers Group, 345 Hudson Street, New York, New York 10014. PSS! is a registered trademark of Penguin Group (USA) Inc. Printed in the U.S.A.

ISBN 978-0-8431-7302-4

10 9 8 7 6 5 4 3 2 1

ALWAYS LEARNING

Theme Song

It's Adventure Time,

C'mon grab your friends,

We'll go to very distant lands.

With Jake the Dog and

Finn the Human,

The fun will never end.

It's Adventure Time!

Fry Song

Daddy, why did you eat my fries?

I bought them, and they were mine.

But you ate them, yeah, you ate my fries.

And I cried, but you didn't see me cry.

Daddy, do you even love me?

Well, I wish you would show it,

'Cause I wouldn't know it.

What kind of dad eats his daughter's fries—

And doesn't even look her in the eyes?

Daddy, there were tears there.

If you saw them, would you even care?

These Lumps

These lumps.

I know you wanna slump up on . . .

These lumps,

But you can't 'cause you're a chump!

A chuuuuuuuuuump!

I'm Just Your Problem

La-da-da-da-da,

I'm gonna bury you in the ground,

La-da-da-da-da,

I'm gonna bury you with my sound,

I'm gonna drink the red from your pretty pink face,

I'm gonna . . .

PB: Marceline, that's too distasteful!

Oh, you don't like that?

Or do you just not like me?!

Sorry I don't treat you like a goddess,

Is that what you want me to do?

Sorry I don't treat you like you're perfect,

Like all your little loyal subjects do.

Sorry I'm not made of sugar,

Am I not sweet enough for you?

Is that why you always avoid me?

That must be such an inconvenience to you.

Well . . . I'm just your problem,

I'm just your problem,

It's like I'm not even a person, am I?

I'm just your problem.

Well, I-I-I-I-I-I-I shouldn't have to justify what I do.

I-I-I-I-I-I-I shouldn't have to prove anything to you.

I'm sorry that I exist.

I forget what landed me on your blacklist,

But I-I-I-I-I-I-I shouldn't have to be the one

that makes up with you,

So . . . why do I want to?

Why do I want to . . .

To . . . bury you in the ground,

And drink the blood from your . . .

Ugh!

Remember You

Marceline: Marceline, is it just you and me

in the wreckage of the world?

That must be so confusing for a little girl.

And I know you're going to need me here with you.

But I'm losing myself, and I'm afraid you're gonna

lose me, too.

This magic keeps me alive,

But it's making me crazy,

And I need to save you,

But who's going to save me?

Please forgive me for whatever I do,

When I don't remember you.

Ice King: Marceline, I can feel myself slipping away.

I can't remember what it made me say.

But I remember that I saw you frown.

I swear it wasn't me, it was the crown.

Together: This magic keeps me alive,

But it's making me crazy.

And I need to save you,

But who's going to save me?

Please forgive me for whatever I do,

When I don't remember you.

Please forgive me for whatever I do,

When I don't remember you.

La-ah-da-da-da-da-da-da,

Da-da-da-da-da-da,

Da-da-da-da-da-da.

"Memory of a Memory"
Baby Finn Song

I'm a buff baby that can dance like a man,

I can shake-ah my fanny, I can shake-ah my can!

I'm a tough tootin' baby, I can punch-ah yo' buns!

Punch-ah yo' buns! I can punch all yo' buns!

If you're an evil witch, I will punch you for fun!

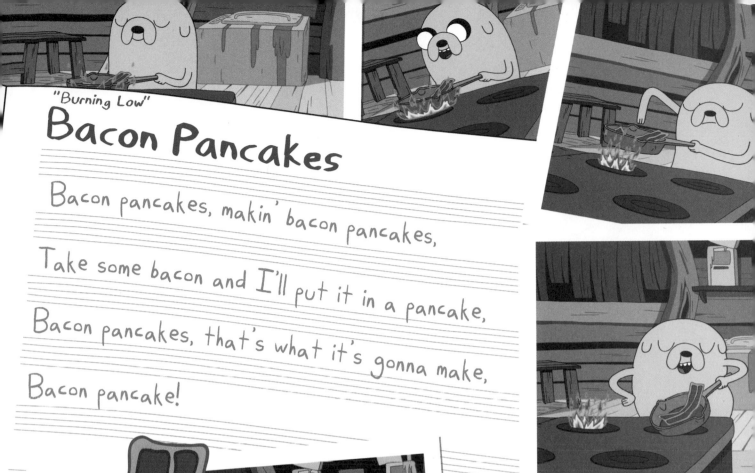

"Burning Low"
Bacon Pancakes

Bacon pancakes, makin' bacon pancakes,

Take some bacon and I'll put it in a pancake,

Bacon pancakes, that's what it's gonna make,

Bacon pancake!

My Best Friends in the World

Everyone . . . Bubblegum . . . I'm so dumb . . .

I should have just told you

What I lost . . . was a piece of your hair.

Now it's gone—gone forever,

But I guess, what does it matter

When I just . . . just had all of you there?

Oh, I just had all of you there with me, my friends . .

If you're even my friends.

You like this? This is what was missing! The truth!

What am I to you?

Am I a joke, your knight, or your brother?

What am I to you?

Do you look down on me 'cause I'm younger?

Do you think that I don't understand?

I just wanted us together and to play as a band,

Last night was the most fun I've ever had,

Even liked it when the two of you would get mad . . .

at each other.

Oh, you a-a-a-a-are my best friends in the world.

You a-a-a-a-are my best friends in the world.

That's ri-i-i-i-ight, I'm talking about the two of

you girls,

And you, Jake.

I wanna sing a song to you, and I refuse to make it fake.

What am I to you?

Am I a joke, your knight, or your brother?

What am I to you?

Do you look down on me 'cause I'm younger?

Do you think that I don't understand?

I just wanted us together and to play as a band.

I'll forget that I lost a piece of your hair,

I'll remember the pasta that we shared . . . over there.

Ah-ah, you a-a-a-a-are my best friends in the world.

You a-a-a-a-are my best friends in the world.

And that's ri-i-i-i-ight, I'm talking about the two

of you girls,

And you, Jake.

I'm gonna sing a song to you, and I refuse to make

it fake.

Make no mistake,

I'm gonna sing a song that feels so real, it'll make

this do-o-o-or break!

Oh, Fionna

I feel like nothing was real until I met you.

I feel like we connect, and I really get you.

If I said, "You're a beautiful girl," would it

upset you?

Because the way you look tonight, silhouetted,

I'll never forget it.

Oh, oh, Fionna.

Your fist has touched my heart.

Oh, oh, Fionna.

I won't let anything in this world keep us apart.

Prince Gumball & Fionna: I won't let

anything in this world keep us apart.

All Gummed Up Inside

I can't keep pushing this down any deeper,

Why do I keep trying if I can't keep her?

Every move I make

Is just another mistake,

I wonder what it would take,

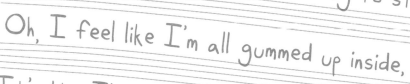

Because it feels like there's a hole inside my body,

Like there's a hole inside my heart.

It's like this feeling is gonna consume me,

If I keep waiting for this thing to start.

Oh, I feel like I'm all gummed up inside,

It's like I'm all gummed up inside,

It's like I'm all gummed up insi-i-i-i-i-ide . . . . .

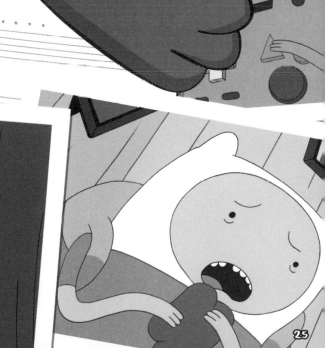

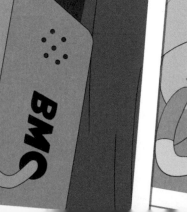

All Warmed Up Inside

Oh, Flame Princess,

I think you're rad.

I really wanna kiss you,

Right in front of your dad.

'Cause I think you're great,

I wanna be your mate,

or maybe go on a date.

'Cause it feels like there's a fire inside my body,

Like there's a fire inside my heart.

It's like this fire is gonna consume me,

If I keep waiting for this thing to start.

Oh, I feel like I'm all warmed up inside,

I feel all warmed up inside,

I feel all warmed up insi-i-i-i-i-ide.

"The Jiggler"

Baby

Finn: Baby, (**Jake:** Ooo!)

Finn: I know what you need,

(**Jake:** What's that?)

Finn: You want your little baby socks . . .

for your little baby feet. (**Jake:** Woooo.)

Finn: Baby, (**Jake:** Yeah?)

Finn: I know what you crave,

(**Jake:** Oh yeah? What's that?)

Finn: You want to poop your pants all day long,

well baby behave!

Finn: Baby . . . you lookin' so good,

You lookin' like you might . . . want some baby food.

(**Jake:** Keep it goin', man!)

Finn: Baby, you lookin' so fine.

You lookin' like you might. . .just start cryin'.

Finn: I gotta tuck you in, girl.

I gotta sing you sweet melodies about babies, yeah!

(**Jake:** Little baby feet!)

"Belly of the Beast"

Bears

Party Pat: Yeah, Yeah, Yeah!

So turn up the music and we'll never leave!

Finn and Jake: Better believe!

Party Pat: We'll never run from the fun,

because we're . . .

Finn and Jake: Bears! Bears! Bears!

Bears! Bears! Bears! Bears! Bears! Bears!

Bears! Bears! Bears! Bears- Beaaaaaaaaaaaaaaa

aaaaaaaaaaaaaaaaaaaaaaaaaaaaaaaaaaaaaaaa

aaaaaaaaaaaaaaaaaaaaaaaaaaaaaaaaaaaaaaaa

aaaaaaaaaarrrrrrrrrrrrrrrrrrrrrrrrrrrrrrrrrrrrrrrr

rrrrrrrrrrrrrrrrrrrrrssssssssssssssssssssssssssssssssss.

"His Hero"

Billy's Song

Who's the greatest warrior ever?

A hero of renown?

Who slayed an evil ocean?

Who cast the Lich King down?

Billy!

And that time the evil Fire Count

Captured a damsel fair.

Who saved her with such brav'ry

She offered him her hair?

Billy!

Also . . . he fought a bear!

Billy!

Dream of Love

Tree Trunks: Dream of love,

Is it really over?

Can I overcome these tears?

I close my eyes,

Feel that he's still with me,

Still standing with me here.

Pig: Dream of love,

Are we truly parted?

Must this pig forever walk alone?

In my dreams,

Our love is just a dream to me.

But in my heart,

It lives and breathes and grows.

Tree Trunks: And even though,

We ain't allowed to be together,

I cross my heart

And promise to be true.

Pig: Well, I'm still lovin' you, girl

From halfway-cross this great, big world,

And in my dreams, I'm holding hands with you.

Both: Dream of love,

Dream of love,

It's only a dream of love,

Dream of love,

Dream of lo-o-ove,

It's only a dream . . . of love.

Tree Trunks: I close my eyes,

And feel his arms around me.

In my dreams,

He's not so far away.

Extremities Song

Shake your extremities!

Shake your extremities!

All your arms and knees,

I want 'em, shake 'em, baby, please!

Baby, shake your eyes for me!

Shake your eyes for me!

Shake your eyes for me!

Shake your eyes for freeee!

Now make some bills,

Make duck bills,

Make a mill,

Quack me up with some yokes,

I like girls who know the ropes,

I like girls who can cope with

the futuristic sound . . . of balloon music.

Friends

Finn, why are you fighting with your friend?

Jake, you know, this can be the end.

Romance or action, does not matter,

Hurting your friends will make you sadder.

Guys, you know you're much more than this.

You two please stop, or you'll undo

All that you've been through.

Just hug and it's agreed,

Your love will not delete.

House Hunting Song

So Finn and Jake

Set out to find a new home.

It's gonna be tough

For a kid and a dog on their own.

Here's a little house,

Aw, Finn's stickin' his foot in.

Well, that's a bad idea, dude,

Cause now that bird thinks you're a jerk, Finn!

And now they're chillin' on the side of a hill!

And thinkin' livin' in a cloud'd be totally thrillin',

Unless they find something inside

Like a mean cloud man and his beautiful cloud bride.

A beehive, oh noooooooooo!

Don't put your foot in there, guy!

Y'all tried that before,

And you know it didn't turn out right!

Big shell, go inside.

Look around, it seems all right.

Frog jumps out and barfs a tiger!

Throwin' down potions for food and fire!

You know you should have stayed

And fought that sexy vampire lady.

Jake was feeling terrified,

He was superscared of her vampire bite,

Which is understandable,

'Cause vampires are really powerful.

They're unreasonable

And burned-out on dealing with mortals.

Oh, Marceline,

Why are you so mean?

Marceline: I'm not mean, I'm a thousand years old,

And I just lost track of my moral code.

Oh, Marceline,

Can't you see these guys are in pain?

Marceline: No, I can't.

I'm invested in this very cute video game.

So there go our boys,

Walkin' on the icy ground.

Headin' toward their destiny,

I'm sure they'll figure something out.

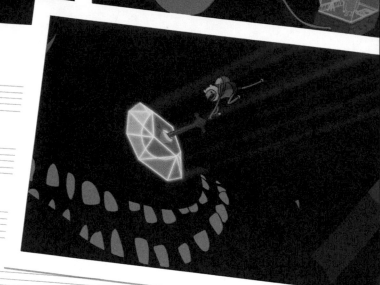

This dungeon, for you!

This world, for you!

This message, it's for you!

Finn!

You're gonna do great, great, great!

You're gonna do great things, things.

You're gonna do great, great, great!

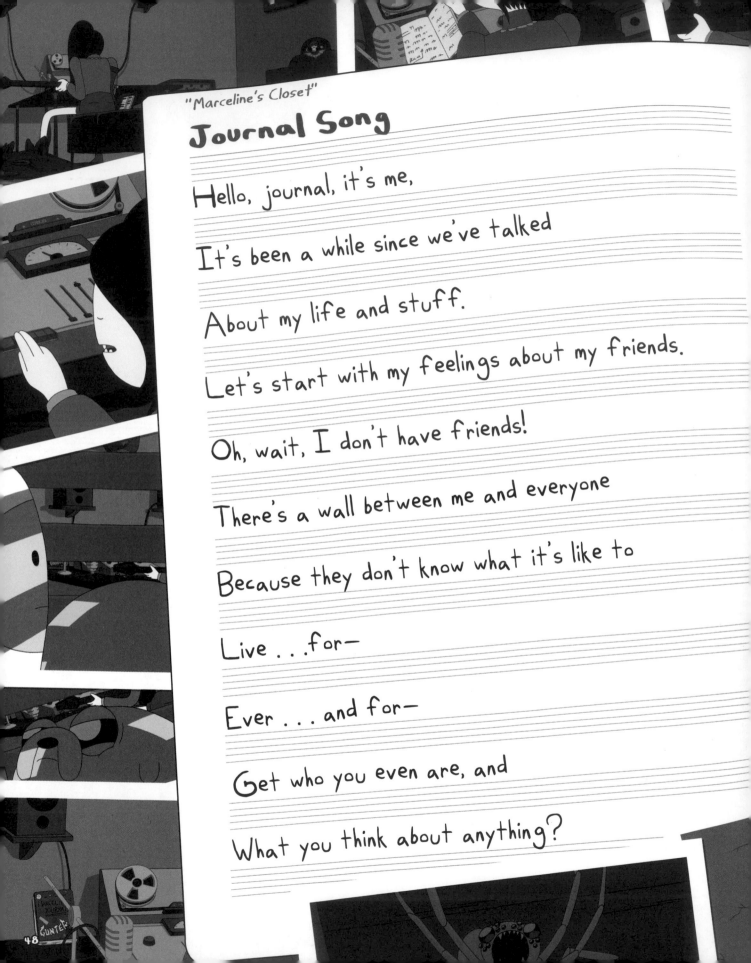

"Marceline's Closet"

Journal Song

Hello, journal, it's me,

It's been a while since we've talked

About my life and stuff.

Let's start with my feelings about my friends.

Oh, wait, I don't have friends!

There's a wall between me and everyone

Because they don't know what it's like to

Live ...for—

Ever ... and for—

Get who you even are, and

What you think about anything?

How can anyone relate to me

When they cannot see what I see?

My vampire eyes see only blood . . . red . . . skies;

Bloodred skies make tears inside that I always hide.

So, I walk alone . . .

In . . . my . . . mental home,

I can't let on . . .

Let Me Show You Something Special

Let me show you something special.

I can introduce your parts to something new.

Every moment now is . . . special.

Just as long as I am spending it with you . . .

You and you and you.

Ice King on tape: There is so much beauty

in this land of ice.

The air is cold, but my feelings feel so warm and nice.

Both: Every turn and spin

Will remind us where we've been.

Will remind us when we found something special.

Will remind us when we found something special.

"Another Way"

Melons

I was wrong.

Was I wrong?

No.

Yes . . . Yes . . .

I was wrong.

How could it be?

I trusted in my guts,

but ended up all nuts.

I was wrong.

How could it be?

Listened to my brain,

But ended up insane.

The melons rolled

Over that lady.

I went too far.

How could it be?

How did I go . . . too far?

Not Just Your Little Girl

I know you just wanna give your little girl the world

But, Daddy, I'm not just your little girl.

I got my own life,

I got my own plans,

I hope you understand . . .

And like the way that I am

'Cause I want your respect, and I wanna be here,

But I don't want to rule the Nightosphere.

Oh, Bubblegum

Slime Princess, you're all right!

Flame Princess, you're okay.

Wildberry Princess could be better.

All of the princesses are pretty all right, but . . .

Oh, Bubblegum!

You look like a lot of fun!

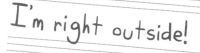

I'm right outside!

And that is how I know.

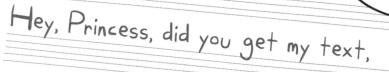

Hey, Princess, did you get my text,

With a picture of my awesome gun show?

I'm also working on my pecs!

If you like, I'll send ya a picture of that, too.

"Morituri Te Salutamus"

On a Tropical Island

As a tropical island,

As a tropical island,

As a tropical island,

As a tropical island.

On a tropical island,

Underneath a molten-lava moon.

Hangin' with the hula dancers,

Askin' questions cause' they got all the answers.

Puttin' on lotion!

Sittin' by the ocean!

Rubbin' it on my body!

Rubbin' it on my body!

Get me out of this caaave,

'Cause it's nothing but a gladiator graaave.

And if I stick to the plaaan,

I think I'll turn into a lava maaan.

I think I'll turn into a lava man!

Susan Strong

Susan Strong,

This is where you belong,

Hangin' with me

On a fallen tree.

Don't you think you deserve this?

To live up here on the surface?

I think you do,

And I think all your friends do, too!

How long have you lived in the darkness?

I just want to show you the light!

Because you're a human, just like me, Susan,

And I want you in my life.

Susan Strong,

You turn my heart on!

"Belly of the Beast"

The Stuff Song

Finn: My hot dog's dead.

My pizza's dead.

My cupcake is dead.

Jake: Oh, uh, my doughnut's dead.

My burger's dead.

My milkshake is dead.

Finn: All of our favorite foods are totally dead.

They can not procreate in little food beds.

We'll eat them up

And turn them into stuff.

Jake: And we'll cry over their graves,

But you can't cry enough . . .

Together: When you miss someone you love

You can't cry enough.

Ending Theme

Come along with me

And the butterflies and bees,

We can wander through the forest

And do so as we please.

Come along with me

To a cliff under a tree.